LIZZY'S LION

L I O N

DENNIS LEE

ILLUSTRATED BY MARIE~LOUISE GAY

LIZZY'S LION

DENNIS LEE

ILLUSTRATED BY MARIE~LOUISE GAY

Stoddart

Lizzy had a lion
    With a big, bad roar,
And she kept him in the bedroom
    By the closet-cupboard door.

Lizzy's lion wasn't friendly,
Lizzy's lion wasn't tame —
Not unless you learned to call him
By his Secret Lion Name.

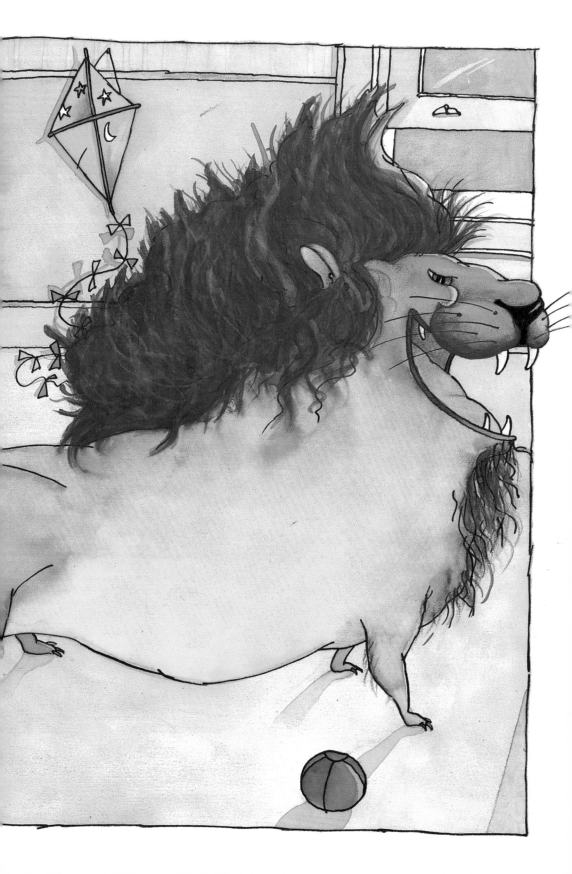

One dark night, a rotten robber
   With a rotten robber mask
Snuck in through the bedroom window —
   And he didn't even ask.

And he brought a bag of candy
That was sticky-icky-sweet,
Just to make friends with a lion
(If a lion he should meet).

First he sprinkled candy forwards,
    Then he sprinkled candy back;
Then he picked up Lizzy's piggy-bank
    And stuck it in his sack.

But as the rotten robber
    Was preparing to depart,
Good old Lizzy's lion wakened
    With a snuffle and a start.

And he muttered, "Candy ? — piffle!"
    And he rumbled, "Candy ? — pooh!"
And he gave the rotten robber
    An experimental chew.

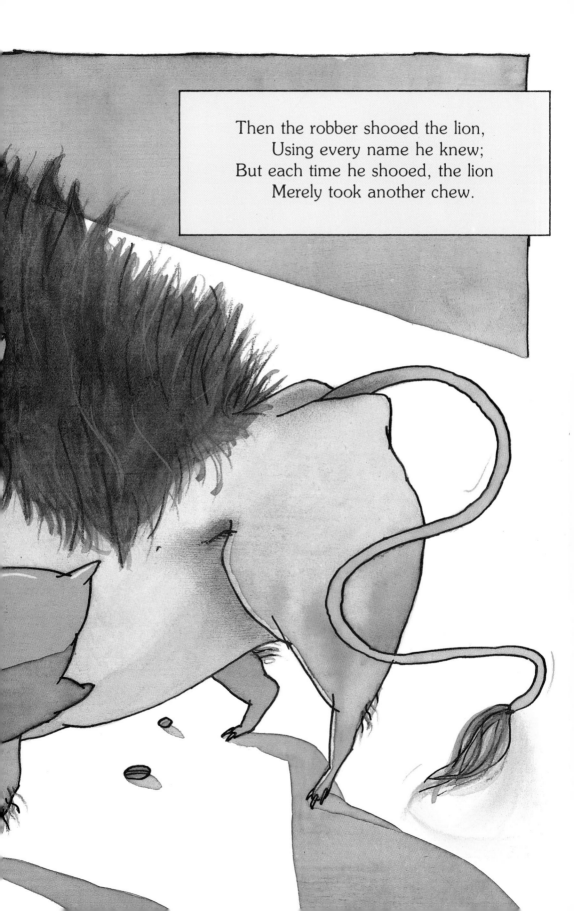

Then the robber shooed the lion,
  Using every name he knew;
But each time he shooed, the lion
  Merely took another chew.

It was: "Down, Fido! Leave, Leo!
Shoo, you good old boy!"
But the lion went on munching
With a look of simple joy.

It was: "Stop, Mopsy! Scram, Sambo!
    This is a disgrace!"
But the lion went on lunching
    With a smile upon his face.

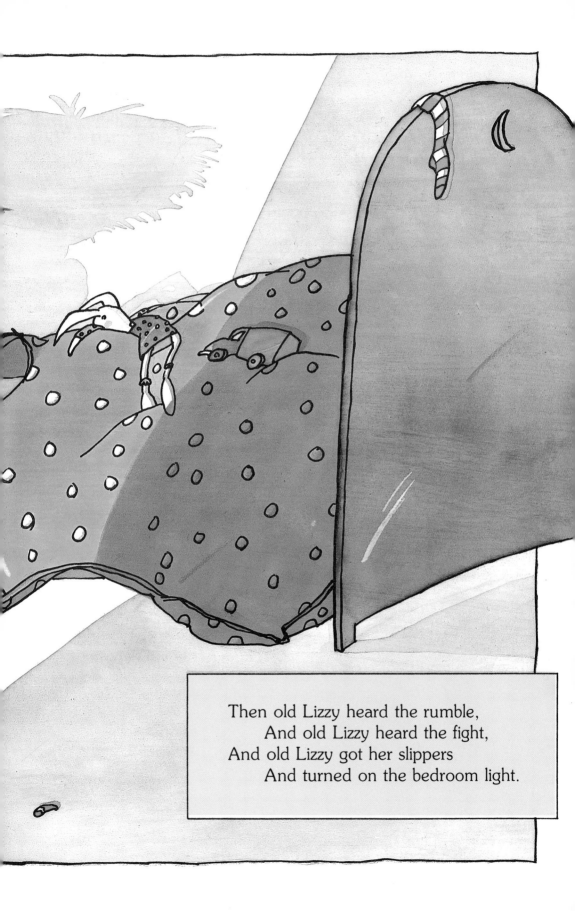

Then old Lizzy heard the rumble,
   And old Lizzy heard the fight,
And old Lizzy got her slippers
   And turned on the bedroom light.

There was robber on the toy-shelf!
There was robber on the rug!
There was robber in the lion
(Who was looking rather smug)!

But old Lizzy wasn't angry,
   And old Lizzy wasn't rough.
She simply said the Secret Name:
   "*Lion!* — that's enough."

Then old Lizzy and her Lion
    Took the toes & tum & head,
And they put them in the garbage,
    And they both went back to bed.

Paperback edition published in 1993 by
Stoddart Publishing Co. Limited
34 Lesmill Road
Toronto, Canada
M3B 2T6
(416) 445-3333

Hardcover edition published in 1984 by
Stoddart Publishing Co. Limited

Canadian Cataloguing in Publication Data

Lee, Dennis, 1939-
   Lizzy's Lion

Poems.
ISBN 0-7736-0078-1 (bound)
ISBN 0-7736-7397-0 (pbk.)

1. Gay, Marie-Louise. II. Title.

PS8523.E4L59 1984   jC811'.54
C84-098890-7   PZ8.3.L43Li 1984

Printed and bound in Canada

*Stoddart Publishing gratefully acknowledges the
support of the Canada Council, Ontario Ministry of
Culture and Communications, Ontario Arts Council,
and Ontario Publishing Centre in the development
of writing and publishing in Canada.*